DATE DUE

JAN 3 0 2003	OCT 1 7 2003	
FEB 0 7 200	MAR 0 4 2004	
	SEP 0 7 2004	
FEB 1 4 2003	OCT 0 7 2004	
FEB 2 6 2003		
MAR 1 0 2003	JAN 2 7 2005	
MAY 3 0 200	MAR 1 6 2005	
SEP 2 4 2003		
OCT 1 6 2003		
APR 0 4 2005		

E
MAR
(orange)

Margulies, Teddy
Clifford the big red dog. The
show . . .

FLOWERY ELEMENTARY SCHOOL

Clifford THE BIG RED DOG®

The SHOW-and-TELL SURPRISE

Adapted by Teddy Margulies

Illustrated by Steve Haefele

**Based on the Scholastic book series
"Clifford The Big Red Dog"
by Norman Bridwell**

From the television script
"Best Friends" by Lois Becker and Mark Stratton

Cartwheel
·B·O·O·K·S·®

SCHOLASTIC INC.

New York   Toronto   London   Auckland   Sydney   Mexico City
New Delhi   Hong Kong

No part of this publication may be reproduced, or stored in a retrieval system, or transmitted in any form or by any means, electronic, mechanical, photocopying, recording, or otherwise, without written permission of the publisher. For information regarding permission, write to Scholastic Inc., Attention: Permissions Department, 555 Broadway, New York, NY 10012.

ISBN 0-439-21359-2

Library of Congress Cataloging-in-Publication Data available

10 9 8 7 6 5 4 3 2 1   01 02 03 04 05

Printed in the U.S.A.   14
First printing, February 2001

Emily Elizabeth looked

up from her desk.

She heard a rumble.

She felt the room shake.

Emily Elizabeth knew what that meant.

So did everyone in her class.

"Here comes Clifford,"

they all yelled.

"It's time to go home."

"Don't forget. Monday

is show-and-tell,"

Miss Carrington said.

"I am going to bring
something cool from
Jamaica," Charley said.

"I am going to bring

something really special,"

Jetta boasted.

Emily Elizabeth did not say anything. She did not know what to bring.

Emily Elizabeth and Clifford

went to the beach

to look for something

special.

While Emily Elizabeth looked,

Clifford dug.

He dug and he dug.

And he dug!

"What a special anchor!"

Emily Elizabeth said.

"My class will love it."

Jetta sniffed.

"That is just like the
anchor I brought for
show-and-tell *last* year."

"Oh, Clifford," Emily Elizabeth sighed.

"We must find something

special on this beach."

Then Emily Elizabeth looked down.

And Clifford looked up.

Up, up, up!

"Wow!" Emily Elizabeth cried.

Clifford lifted her

to the top of a cliff.

On the cliff was
an old nest.
It still had some feathers
and eggshells inside.

"This will be great for
show-and-tell," Emily Elizabeth said.
Clifford said, "Woof!"
and poked his nose
into the nest.

"Oh, no," Emily Elizabeth said.

Then she giggled.

Clifford looked so funny.

Emily Elizabeth left the beach
and went to town.
"Maybe Mom has something
special in her shop,"
she told Clifford.

Emily Elizabeth came out of

the shop with a coral necklace.

But it wasn't as special as

Jetta's coral statue.

Emily Elizabeth felt like crying.

But she laughed

when she saw what

Clifford was doing.

"Come on," she said.

"Let's get a snack."

Emily Elizabeth saw Charley.

"Did you find something

for show-and-tell?"

Emily Elizabeth asked him.

"I'm bringing my steel drum," he said. "What are you bringing?"

"I don't know," Emily Elizabeth said.

"Clifford and I spent the whole day

looking for something.

"We went swinging

and cliff-climbing

and shopping

in town.

But we did not find

anything special."

"That sounds like fun, though,"
Charley said. "Clifford is a cool dog."
"He sure is," Emily Elizabeth said.

"Well, I hope you
find something
for show-and-tell,"
Charley said.

"Thanks," Emily Elizabeth
said. "I think I just did."

On Monday, Emily Elizabeth
showed up for show-and-tell.
She was not alone.
"Hooray! It's Clifford!"
everyone cheered.

But Jetta did not.

"I knew you would bring

that big old red dog,"

she said.

Emily Elizabeth grinned.

"Of course," she said.

"Clifford is really special!"

Do You Remember?

Circle the right answer.

1. What was in the nest?
   a. Peanut butter and jelly.
   b. Feathers and seashells.
   c. Feathers and eggshells.

2. What did Clifford and Emily Elizabeth do in town?
   a. They went shipping.
   b. They went chopping.
   c. They went shopping.

Which happened first?
Which happened next?
Which happened last?
Write a 1, 2, or 3 in the space after each sentence.

Emily Elizabeth brought Clifford to show-and-tell. _____

Clifford dug a hole. _____

Clifford found an anchor. _____

Answers:

Clifford found an anchor. (2)
Clifford dug a hole. (1)
Emily Elizabeth brought Clifford to show-and-tell. (3)
1-c; 2-c.